AMY ELIZABETH EXPLORES BLOOMINGDALE'S

Thank you to:

Margie DeWitt for being Grandma,
Helene Edwards for telling me what
 the title of my next book should be,
Judy Johnson for Chuck,
 and

Atheneum   Maxwell Macmillan Canada, Inc.
Macmillan Publishing Company   1200 Eglinton Avenue East
866 Third Avenue   Suite 200
New York, NY 10022   Don Mills, Ontario M3C 3N1

Macmillan Publishing Company is part of the Maxwell Communication Group of Companies.

First edition

Printed in Hong Kong by South China Printing Company (1988) Ltd.

10 9 8 7 6 5 4 3 2 1

The text of this book is set in 14/16 Aster.

Library of Congress Cataloging-in-Publication Data

Konigsburg, E. L.
    Amy Elizabeth explores Bloomingdale's / by E.L. Konigsburg.
        p.   cm.
    Summary: The many sights of New York provide daily distractions for
Amy Elizabeth and Grandma as they attempt to find the time to go see Bloomingdale's.
    ISBN 0–689–31766–2
    [1. New York (N.Y.)—Fiction. 2. Grandmothers—Fiction.]
I. Title.
PZ7.K8352Am   1992
[E]—dc20   91–40132

A Jean Karl Book

ATHENEUM   1992   NEW YORK

MAXWELL MACMILLAN CANADA
Toronto

MAXWELL MACMILLAN INTERNATIONAL
New York   Oxford   Singapore   Sydney

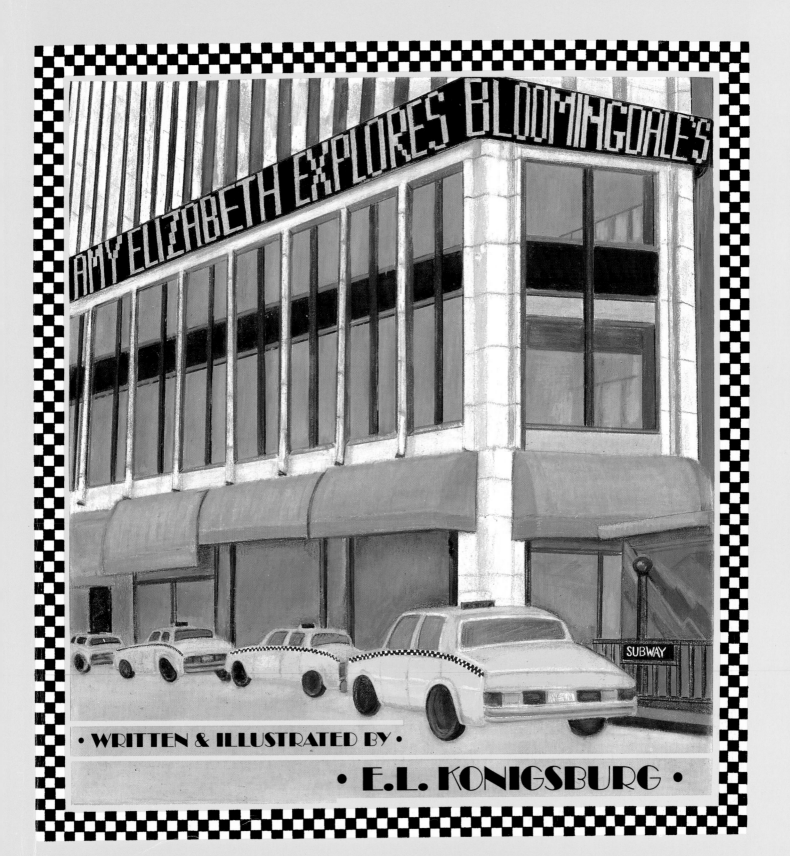

AMY ELIZABETH EXPLORES BLOOMINGDALE'S

SUBWAY

• WRITTEN & ILLUSTRATED BY •

• E.L. KONIGSBURG •

ON THE FIRST DAY of my visit, my grandma said to me, "Today we will go to Bloomingdale's—we New Yorkers call it *Bloomie's*. It is the most famous store in the world. But first we must take Alexander the Great for a walk."

Grandma took her coat from the peg, her hat from the rack, her scarf and gloves from the drawer, and a pooper-scooper from the closet.

In Houston, people who have pets don't have pooper-scoopers because they have lawns.

There were hundreds of
people in the streets carrying
hundreds of signs.
Grandma said, "This is a
protest march, Amy
Elizabeth."
I explained to Grandma
that in Houston when people
march and carry signs,
there is also a band,
and it is a parade.
By the time we got back to
Grandma's apartment, it was
too late to get to Bloomingdale's.

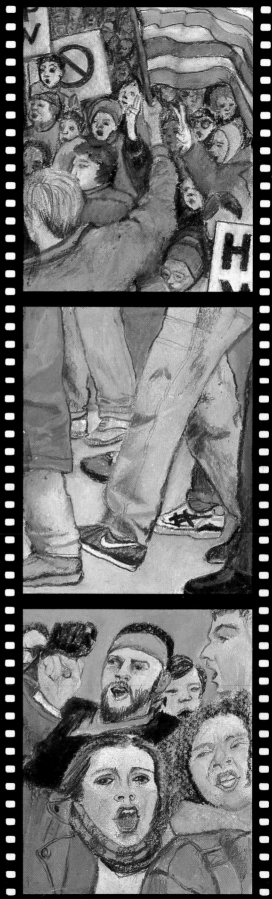

O N THE SECOND DAY of my visit, my grandma said to me, "Today we will go to Bloomingdale's, but first we must take the downtown train—we New Yorkers call it the *subway*—to buy some green tea and gingerroot."

Grandma took her coat from the peg, her hat from the rack, her scarf and gloves from the drawer, and two subway tokens from her pocketbook.

In Houston trains don't ride under the town. In Houston trains come and go from out of town, and they ride on top, the same as cars and trucks.

There were hundreds of people on the sidewalks selling hundreds of things, and there were hundreds of people buying them.

Grandma said, "This is part of New York City, Amy Elizabeth. We New Yorkers call it *Chinatown*."

I explained to Grandma that in Houston there are no foreign towns. In my town, Chinatown would be in another country like China. I also explained that in Houston all the signs—even the ones in Spanish—are spelled out in English.

By the time we got back to Grandma's apartment, it was too late to get to Bloomingdale's.

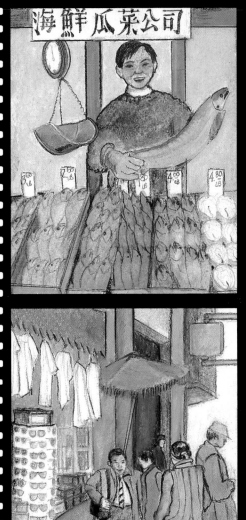

ON THE THIRD DAY of my visit, my grandma said to me, "Today we will go to Bloomingdale's. We'll take the city bus." Grandma took her coat from the peg, her hat from the rack, her scarf and gloves from the drawer, and a lot of change from her pocketbook, because you need exact change to ride the city bus.

In Houston I don't know if you need exact change to ride the city bus because we live so far from the bus stop that we have to drive to get there, so we drive the rest of the way as well.

Grandma said, "No one drives in New York City, Amy Elizabeth. There's too much traffic."

There were hundreds of cars with hundreds of drivers who didn't know that no one drives in New York City. The bus had to stop because of an accident caused by two of them.

Grandma said, "This is the Empire State Building, Amy Elizabeth. Not long ago and for a very long time, it was the tallest building in the world."

I don't know what else it is, but in Houston we would call it a restaurant. Houston has hundreds of restaurants, and all their signs, spelled out in English, say the same thing—R-E-S-T-A-U-R-A-N-T— unless they say McDonald's.

Grandma said, "We're going to be stuck in traffic a long time, Amy Elizabeth. We might as well get off the bus and go to the top of the Empire State Building and have a look around."

Grandma paid—exact change not required—and we rode an elevator to the top.

In Houston we don't have pay elevators.

I looked around, but I didn't see Bloomie's. I saw Macy's. Houston has a Macy's. I saw hundreds of tall buildings, some bridges, two rivers, and a very large park. I also saw New Jersey. I did not know that New York City had so much geography.

Grandma said, "Bloomie's is just around the corner from those tall buildings, Amy Elizabeth, and if they weren't in the way, we could see it."

By the time we got back down on the ground, it was too late to get to Bloomingdale's.

ON THE FOURTH DAY of my visit, my grandma said to me, "Today we will do the laundry."

I asked Grandma if there is no Bloomingdale's on Thursdays.

Grandma said, "On Thursday, Amy Elizabeth, Bloomingdale's is open late, so after we do the laundry, we can have an early supper at the Carnegie Delicatessen—we New Yorkers call it the *Carnegie Deli*—and then go on to Bloomie's."

Grandma took her coat from the peg, her hat from the rack, her scarf and gloves from the drawer, and a two-wheeler shopping cart from the back of the closet.

There were hundreds of washers and hundreds of dryers. Grandma used three of each.

In Houston we don't have to leave home to do the laundry. We do it one load at a time and don't watch.

The Carnegie Deli is a R-E-S-T-A-U-R-A-N-T. Grandma said, "We'll share a hot pastrami sandwich and an order of potato pancakes with applesauce."

I explained to Grandma that in Houston I order my own sandwich—a hamburger. I also explained that in Houston I take my potatoes french fried and my pancakes with syrup for breakfast.

The pickles were already on the tables. They were free. Some of the pickles were green tomatoes. I am a child who enjoys a good pickle. I ate hundreds of the green tomato ones.

I could not finish the potato pancakes. I could not start half of the hot pastrami sandwich. Grandma said, "You are turning as green as a green tomato pickle, Amy Elizabeth. I think we better return to my apartment."

The waiter wrapped up my half of the hot pastrami sandwich, and when we got back to the apartment, Grandma gave it to Alexander the Great and gave me green tea from Chinatown to settle my stomach, and it was too late to get to Bloomingdale's.

ON THE FIFTH DAY of my visit, my grandma said to me, "Today we will go to Bloomingdale's, but first we will take a hansom ride around Central Park, and then we'll walk over to Bloomie's, which is only three city blocks away."

I did not know what a hansom is, so I did not know if we have them in Houston.

Grandma took her coat from the peg, her hat from the rack, her scarf and gloves from the drawer, and snow boots from the back of the closet. In a hundred years it only snowed once in Houston, so I didn't bring my snow boots to New York because I don't have them.

Hansoms are buggies pulled by horses that wear diapers. Houston doesn't have them.

It started to snow. Big wet snowflakes flew all around.

I did not explain that I was very cold. I also did not explain that my feet without snow boots were frozen into ice.

Grandma said, "You look very cold, Amy Elizabeth, and I'll bet your feet are frozen into ice. We will walk to Rumpelmayer's across the street and have hot chocolate to warm us up, and then we'll go to Bloomingdale's and buy you some snow boots."

Even if you are a child who has never been snowed upon, Rumpelmayer's hot chocolate is an excellent way to warm up.

By the time we drank hot chocolate and were all warmed up, it was too late to get to Bloomingdale's even though it was only three city blocks away, so we returned to the apartment.

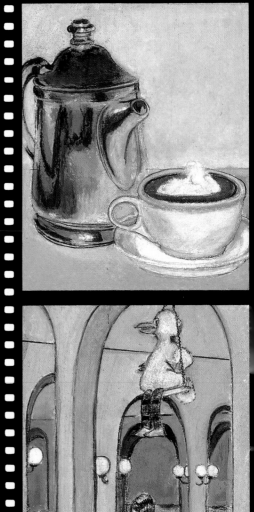

ON THE SIXTH DAY of my visit, my grandma said to me, "Today we will go to Bloomingdale's, but first we will go to see *Peter Pan* because it is Saturday and there will be a matinee."

In Houston we had already rented the tape of *Peter Pan* twice.

Grandma said, "This *Peter Pan* is neither a cartoon nor a movie, Amy Elizabeth. It is live theater. Everything that happens will happen right before your eyes."

Grandma took her coat from the peg, her hat from the rack, her scarf and gloves from the drawer, and a pair of binoculars from the windowsill.

First Peter Pan flew in through the bedroom window right before my eyes, and later Tinker Bell started to die right before my eyes. That's when Peter Pan asked, "Do you believe in fairies? If you believe, clap your hands." I clapped. Grandma did her part, too. She clapped. And right there, right before our eyes, we saved Tinker Bell.

When the theater was over, we went back out into New York City. There were hundreds of grandmothers and primary caregivers trying to get a taxi. By the time one of them stopped for us, it was too late to get to Bloomingdale's.

O N THE SEVENTH DAY of my visit, my grandma said to me, "Today there will be no Bloomingdale's, Amy Elizabeth, because it is Sunday, and we New Yorkers get the Sunday *Times*."

Grandma took her coat from the peg, her hat from the rack, her scarf and gloves from the drawer, and a shopping bag from the closet.

The Sunday *Times* is a newspaper. It has hundreds and hundreds of pages and not one of them is funnies. In Houston we never buy the newspaper. It is thrown onto our driveway every day of the week, including Sunday.

Grandma, Alexander the Great, and I walked to one store for hot bagels, to another for fresh cream cheese and lox, and to the bakery for prune danish. We bought apples from a stand on the corner.

Grandma also bought me flowers.

In all my life in Houston, no one ever bought me flowers.

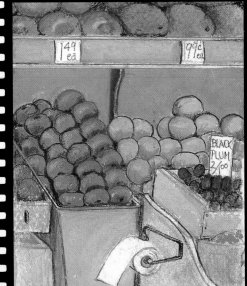

First we ate bagels with cream cheese and lox. The bagels were still warm from the bakery, and my grandma explained that lox is smoked salmon and is salty unless you call it nova.

Then Grandma showed me a picture in the Sunday *Times.* There in black and white was the person who played Peter Pan at the live theater. Grandma read out loud to me that in real life, Peter Pan is a girl who is as grown-up as my mother, but in the theater she becomes Peter Pan, a boy who never grows up.

I explained to Grandma that in Houston girls don't play at being boys except on Halloween.

Grandma said, "Peter Pan is always played by a girl, Amy Elizabeth. The theater has its own magic."

Grandma read me hundreds of pages from the Sunday *Times,* and I was her live audience, and when her throat got dry from reading out loud, I gave her green tea from Chinatown, and she did the *Times* crossword puzzle.

ON THE LAST DAY of my visit, my grandma said to me, "Today we must go to the airport, Amy Elizabeth, so that Alexander the Great and I can take you back to Houston. I've hired a limousine to take us to the airport. We New Yorkers call it a *limo*."

I explained to Grandma that in Houston we also call it a *limo*. In Houston hundreds of people have them instead of cars.

Grandma took her coat from the peg, her hat from the rack, her scarf and gloves from the drawer, and a suitcase and Alexander the Great's carrying case from the deep closet in her bedroom.

After we drove a while, Grandma asked the driver to take us to Bloomie's. "It is just around the corner," she explained.

The driver said, "Bloomingdale's is not open yet, madam. If we wait for it to open, you will miss your plane."

Grandma said, "Every day we were too late to get to Bloomingdale's, Amy Elizabeth, and today we are too early." I did not explain to Grandma that yesterday we did not try at all.

I remembered the protest march, the subway, the city bus, and the hansom. I remembered Peter Pan. I remembered green tomato pickles, hot chocolate, warm bagels, green tea from Chinatown, and the flowers my grandma gave to me.

The limo went over one of the bridges I had seen from the top of the Empire State Building. I looked out the back window and saw hundreds of buildings moving farther and farther away. One of them was the Empire State Building. Some of them were Chinatown. One was Bloomingdale's.

I said to my grandma, "I have had an excellent time not getting there."

And my grandma explained to me, "That's good to hear, Amy Elizabeth. So have I. So have I."